# Franklin and the Hero

From an episode of the animated TV series *Franklin*
produced by Nelvana Limited, Neurones France s.a.r.l.
and Neurones Luxembourg S.A.

Based on the *Franklin* books by
Paulette Bourgeois and Brenda Clark.

TV tie-in adaptation written by Sharon Jennings
and illustrated by Sean Jeffrey, Mark Koren, Jelena Sisic, and Shelley Southern.

Based on the TV episode *Franklin and the Hero*, written by Shane MacDougall.

Franklin is a trade mark of Kids Can Press Ltd.
Kids Can Press is a Nelvana company.
The character Franklin was created by Paulette Bourgeois and Brenda Clark.

ISBN 0-439-20380-5

12 11 10 9 8 7 6 5 4 3 2 1          0 1 2 3 4 5/0

Printed in the U.S.A.          23

First Scholastic printing, November 2000

# Franklin and the Hero

*Based on characters created by*
*Paulette Bourgeois and Brenda Clark*

SCHOLASTIC INC.

New York   Toronto   London   Auckland   Sydney
Mexico City   New Delhi   Hong Kong

FRANKLIN could count by twos and tie his shoes. He could say the alphabet without stopping, and he was learning how to read. His favorite books were about Dynaroo, the kangaroo superhero. Franklin wanted to be just like Dynaroo.

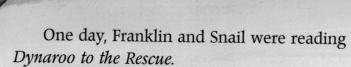

One day, Franklin and Snail were reading
*Dynaroo to the Rescue.*

"Look, Snail," cried Franklin. "Dynaroo pulls Koala
out of the quicksand with one mighty tug!"

"Dynaroo's the best," Snail sighed happily.

Franklin agreed. "I want to be as strong as she is."

"I want to be as fast," said Snail.

Franklin had an idea.

"Let's play superheroes," he suggested. "I'm Turtle-roo, strong enough to lift a truck!"

"And I'm Dyna-snail," announced Snail, "faster than a speeding train!"

"Together we'll keep the world safe," declared Franklin.

"Just like Dynaroo," added Snail.

Turtle-roo and Dyna-snail ran outside. They saved their snow fort from a terrible snow monster over and over again.

Hours later, Franklin's mother called to them. "Turtle-roo! Dyna-snail! Come inside. I have a big surprise."

When the superheroes were warm and dry, Franklin's mother told them the good news.

"Dynaroo will be autographing her new book at Mr. Heron's bookstore tomorrow morning," she said. "Do you know anyone who would like to go?"

Franklin and Snail jumped up and down and gave each other the Dynaroo salute.

For the rest of the afternoon, Franklin and Snail talked about Dynaroo. They reread all of Dynaroo's adventures and made their plans for the next day. They were both so excited they could hardly eat their dinner or fall asleep that night.

Early in the morning, Franklin and Snail set off for the bookstore. As they rounded a bend in the path, they saw Mrs. Muskrat searching through the snow.

"I dropped my house key," she explained. "And now I'm locked out. Can you help me find it?"

Franklin looked at Snail.

"But…" Snail began.

"Come on, Snail," Franklin decided. "This shouldn't take two superheroes long at all."

Franklin was wrong. They dug and dug without finding the key.

"We may not find it until the snow melts," Mrs. Muskrat said finally. "It's time to call off the search."

Franklin and Snail breathed sighs of relief and turned to go.

"If you could pile some snow under the window," continued Mrs. Muskrat, "maybe we could get in that way."

"But, Mrs. Muskrat," Franklin said, then stopped. Mrs. Muskrat was shivering.

So Franklin huffed and puffed and rolled a huge snowball to the kitchen window. He climbed on top and pushed and shoved until the window opened just enough for Snail to crawl through.

Up and over the ledge went Snail, across the counter, down the wall, over the floor, and up the door. Finally, Snail turned the door handle.

"Hurray!" shouted Franklin.

"This calls for hot chocolate and cake!" declared Mrs. Muskrat.

Franklin and Snail looked at the kitchen clock.

"Thank you, Mrs. Muskrat," said Franklin. "But… you see…" And he finally told her all about Dynaroo.

"Well, off you go!" exclaimed Mrs. Muskrat. "I can thank both of you properly another time."

Franklin and Snail hurried to town and rushed into the bookstore.

But no one was there. They had missed Dynaroo.

Franklin's shoulders slumped, and Snail started to cry. As they turned to go, Mr. Heron came out of the back room.

"We've been waiting for you," he said with a smile.

Mr. Heron stepped aside, and there was Dynaroo.
Franklin and Snail gasped in amazement.

"I couldn't leave until I'd met two real-life heroes,"
Dynaroo announced.

Franklin and Snail were confused.

"Mrs. Muskrat phoned and told us what happened,"
explained Mr. Heron. "You are both heroes to her."

"But we were just pretending to be heroes," said Franklin. "Real heroes are superfast and superstrong."

"Sometimes they are," agreed Dynaroo. "But there are other ways to be a hero."

Franklin thought for a moment. Then he smiled.

"I never knew that helping someone could make you a hero," he said.

Dynaroo gave both Franklin and Snail a copy of her new book, *Dynaroo's Jungle Adventure*. Inside each was a dedication from Dynaroo.

Franklin read his aloud. "To Franklin, my heroic friend."

Franklin and Snail gave Dynaroo a big hug, and Mr. Heron took everyone's picture.

Later that night, when Snail's family had left and Mrs. Muskrat's cake was all gone, Franklin went to bed with his new book and a flashlight. He planned to read the whole story. But soon he was sound asleep.

Even superheroes need their rest.